CAPTAIN STUMPY

the Pirate Cat

By Jeremy E. Bliven • Illustrated by Herbert A. Bliven

D1307552

CAPTAIN STUMPY
the Pirate Cat
Jeremy E. Bliven and Herbert A. Bliven

OuterBanks press An Outer Banks Press Book
Published in 2004 by Outer Banks Press, a subsidiary of OBBC, Inc.

Illustrations by Herbert A. Bliven

Cover Design and Book Design by 8 Dot Graphics for Outer Banks Press

ISBN **978-0-9713890-8-X**

Library of Congress Catalog Number: **TXU1-190-314**

Printed by Jones Printing, Chesapeake, Virginia

For bulk purchases, special sales and book signings, please contact:

Outer Banks Press
Post Office Box 2829
Kitty Hawk, North Carolina 27949
252.261.0612
252.261.0613 FAX
mail@outerbankspress.com
www.outerbankspress.com

OUTER BANKS PRESS is an independent publisher specializing in fine magazines and books of literary and photographic merit, distinctive in both content and design.

CAPTAIN STUMPY
the Pirate Cat

For **MICHAEL**, **MATTHEW** and **MADELINE**.
Special thanks to David Guiley and Lauren Quinn.

Captain Stumpy the Pirate Cat
and his crew; **GWEN**, **VAN** and **POP**,

sailed on a pond named the Puddle

to a fish-house with a shark on top.

They called their ship **NICE KITTY**,

the fish-house's name was **JAWS**

and when they pulled up to the dock

they could hear the fishermen call...

*"**RUN FOR YOUR LIVES**. It's Stumpy the Pirate."*

Stumpy smiled and pulled a patch over his eye,

then jumped onto the dock to limp

toward where the huddled fishermen cried.

"Please don't hurt us Captain Stumpy,"

he heard a fisherman say.

Stumpy simply said, *"**ME-ARRRGH**,"*

and went to where the fishes lay.

He took the **BIGGEST TROUT** he could carry

and stumped back to the ship.

But before he made it safely back

he hit some ice and **SLIPPED**.

The fishermen roared with laughter,

because they had always liked Stumpy

and only pretended to be **SCARED**

of the cat whose head was sore and lumpy.

Stumpy stumbled into his cabin
and wouldn't come out for anything;
not for **MILK** or **CHEESE** or **BUTTER**,
not even for a new diamond earring.

Van had been asleep for hours

and Gwen was always hiding,

so Pop raised the **SAILS**, grabbed the **WHEEL**

and set that ship to gliding.

They raced over the open pond

with the wind into their faces

and had almost reached the other side

when Pop screamed, *"Oh my gracious!"*

A ship was coming up astern
with its giant **CANNONS BOOMING**,

so Stumpy ran out on deck

and saw the **DANGER** looming.

"Me-arrrrgh!" Stumpy growled.
"It's that great ball of fur
FLUFF BUCKET *the fish-stealing pirate.*
But he won't get my trout," he purred.

Fluff Bucket had a crew of one,
the giant pirate **TIGGIE PANTS**.
That cat was so blasted big
he made Stumpy's crew look like **ANTS**.

Gwen covered her eyes with her paws,

while Van woke up for a **PEEK**.

Pop **HID** behind the wheel

and Stumpy forgot how to speak.

"*SHIVER ME WHISKERS*," Stumpy stammered.
"*Batten down the bilge pumps.*
Load the crow's nest. Fire the cook..." he managed
before he fell to the deck with a thump.

"Me-hah hah hah," Fluff Bucket laughed,
slapping his fluffy knees.
*"The brave Captain Stumpy's passed out again
and the others would faint if I sneezed."*

Tiggie Pants, as always, just stared at the sky
because he liked the color blue.
Suddenly he roared, *"**ME WANT FISH**,"*
which were the only words he knew.

Hearing that wonderful word, **FISH**,

Captain Stumpy woke in a **DAZE**.

He grabbed a rope to help himself up,

but fell again when a cannon blazed.

Captain Stumpy sat stunned by the noise

because he didn't know what it meant.

Then he saw Fluff Bucket's **SINKING** ship and knew

he'd fired a cannonball by accident.

Gwen, Van and Pop let loose a cheer,

"Captain Stumpy! Captain Stumpy! Hooray!"

as they watched Tiggie Pants walk to shore.

Stumpy smiled and said, ***"YEP, I SAVED THE DAY."***

Fluff Bucket wasn't tall like Tiggie Pants,

so he couldn't just walk to shore.

Plus, he had all that fur

and was glad he hadn't grown any more.

Stumpy stopped smiling when he saw Fluff Bucket,

since most cats don't like water at all.

But he took off his **WOODEN LEG** and his hat

because someone had to save that **FUR-BALL**.

Stumpy flopped in and cat-paddled

to where Fluff Bucket **SPLASHED**.

But some mean fish kept biting his toes

and that made him swim like a flash.

Grabbing Fluff Bucket under his soggy arms,
Stumpy pulled him back to the boat.
Gwen, Van and Pop pulled them in
and Stumpy said, *"Quick, get a coat."*

They wrapped him up tight but he didn't move,
because that poor cat was in **SHOCK**.
Stumpy shook his head and said, *"Let's go!*
We have to get him to the dock."

The fishermen ran out to help

and hauled Fluff and Stump inside

to wrap them in blankets and feed them **WARM MILK**

until they were cozy and dried.

As they sat there alone Fluff Bucket said,
*"Stumpy, do you think we could be **FRIENDS**?"*
"Of course you bucket of fluff," Stumpy replied,
and that made both of them grin.

They thanked the fishermen for all their help
and went to join Gwen, Van and Pop.
"Let's go find Tiggie Pants," Fluff Bucket said,
which made Gwen **FAINT** to the deck with a **PLOP**.

As they sailed off together the fishermen called,
"*Come back whenever you wish.*"

Stumpy smiled and yelled back,

"*Just as long as you* **GIVE ME SOME FISH***.*"

Stumpy

Pop

Gwen

Van

Tiggie Pants

Fluff Bucket